TONI MORRISON
& SLADE MORRISON

Peeny Butter Fudge

Illustrated by
JOE CEPEDA

A PAULA WISEMAN BOOK
SIMON & SCHUSTER BOOKS FOR YOUNG READERS
New York   London   Toronto   Sydney

To Nidal and Safa
—T. M.

To Kali-ma
—S. M.

For my abuelas,
Josefina Cepeda and María Arévalo
—J. C.

SIMON & SCHUSTER BOOKS FOR YOUNG READERS • An imprint of Simon & Schuster Children's Publishing Division • 1230 Avenue of the Americas, New York, New York 10020 • Text copyright © 2009 by Toni Morrison and Slade Morrison • Illustrations copyright © 2009 by Joe Cepeda • All rights reserved, including the right of reproduction in whole or in part in any form. • SIMON & SCHUSTER BOOKS FOR YOUNG READERS is a trademark of Simon & Schuster, Inc. • Book design by Lizzy Bromley • The text for this book is set in Paradigm. • The illustrations for this book are rendered in oil paints. • Manufactured in the United States of America • 2 4 6 8 10 9 7 5 3 1 • Library of Congress Cataloging-in-Publication Data • Morrison, Toni. • Peeny butter fudge / Toni Morrison and Slade Morrison ; illustrated by Joe Cepeda. • p. cm. • "A Paula Wiseman book." • Summary: Children spend the day with their grandmother, who ignores their mother's carefully planned schedule in favor of activities that are much more fun. • ISBN: 978-1-4169-8332-3 (hardcover) • [1. Stories in rhyme. 2. Grandmothers—Fiction.] I. Morrison, Slade. II. Cepeda, Joe, ill. III. Title. • PZ8.3.M836 Pe • [E]—dc22 • 2008052267

first edition

Snuggle, snuggle.
Time to rest.
Nana joins us in her nest.
Nap time, nap time
is not so long
when Nana sings a sleepy song.

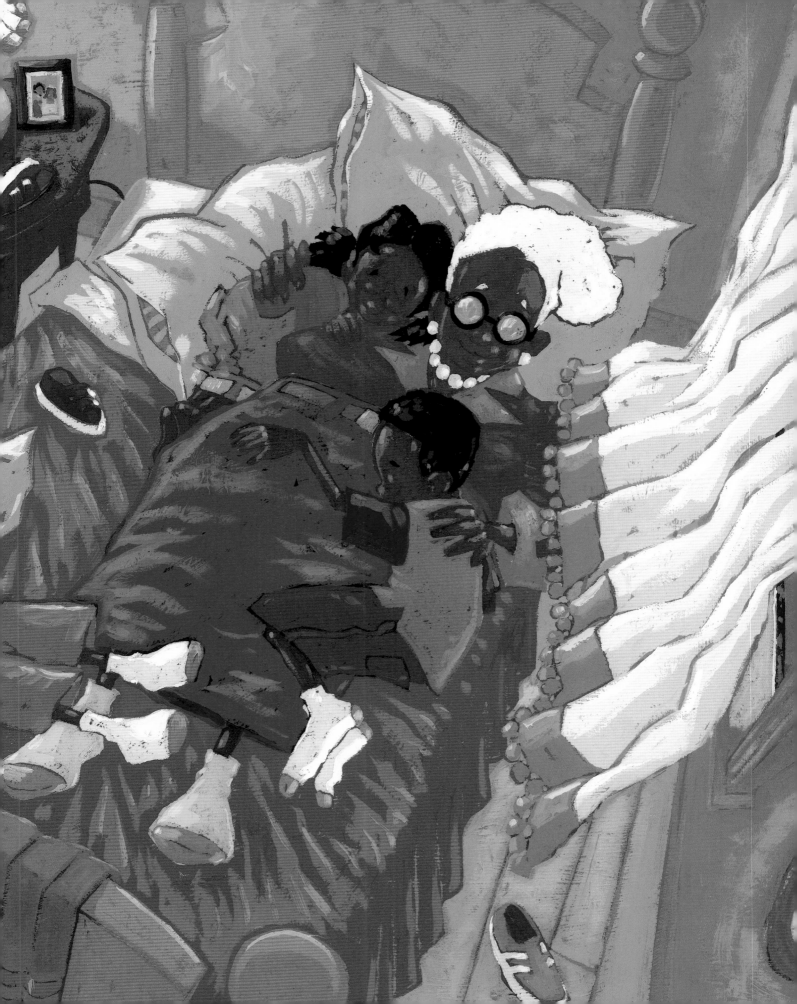

Looky look, looky look,
we get to get a storybook.
Fairies, dragons everywhere.
Creepy things under the stairs.
Pots of gold, a laughing mouse,
a peppermint chimney on a house.

Hurry, hurry,
hop in the car.
Let's go fast, let's go far.
All around, up and down,
Nana takes us through the town.

Yummy, lummy. Yummy, lummy.
So much happy in the tummy.
Look at what our nana made us:
biscuits, ham, and lemonade—us.

Oh my goodness, Nana's sick.
Help! Find the doctor kit.
She's got a fever,
her face is hot.
Get some water,
pour a lot.
Band-Aid for her toes,
Band-Aid for her nose.
Doctor says you need rest.
Quiet while we check your chest.
Be good, Nana.
Take a vitamin pill.
We'll make you well,
you bet we will!

Hold my hand and swing around.
Feel the rhythm in the ground.
Lift your left foot,
now your right.
Shake your shoulders
with all your might.

Let's make the kitty cat.
I've got one paw.
I've got two.
Here's his tail and whiskers, too.
Here's his play toy,
but it doesn't belong.
The shape is right,
but the color is wrong.
Patience, patience.
No need for haste.
Every piece has its place.

Peeny butter fudge,
peeny butter fudge.
Mommy's coming any minute.
Quick, quick. Let's begin it.

Shh, don't tell.
But I can't help it.
This recipe's a family secret.
Mix it, cook it.
Cool it, eat it.
My mother taught me,
and I taught yours.
Don't ever forget how it's done,
for you will have to pass it on.

Ticky-tock, ticky-tock.
Can we beat that big, old clock?
Peeny butter, peeny butter.
Nana is the best grandmother.

Give me a kiss, give me a hug.
Peeny butter, peeny butter,
peeny butter fudge.

Peeny Butter Fudge

Ingredients

1 tablespoon butter

1 cup whole milk

Two 1-ounce squares
    unsweetened chocolate

2 cups sugar

1/4 teaspoon vanilla

1/4 cup creamy peanut
    butter

Equipment

8-inch-square glass cake pan

4-quart saucepan

Wooden spoon

Clear drinking glass,
    filled with cold water

Large pan (or sink),
    filled with cold water

Sharp knife

Please do not attempt this recipe without an adult helper.

Butter the inside of the cake pan; set aside. Combine milk and chocolate squares in the saucepan. Stir over low heat with the wooden spoon until squares begin to melt or have melted completely. Add sugar and stir. Increase heat to medium and let cook, stirring occasionally, until mixture comes to a low boil. After five minutes of boiling, test the mixture's readiness by placing a drop of it into the glass of cold water. Keep doing this until a drop forms a tadpole shape as it falls through the water. Turn off the heat and remove the saucepan from the stove. Add vanilla and stir. Place the saucepan in the large pan or sink of cold water, making sure none of the water enters the saucepan. Let sit. After a few minutes, ask an adult to lift the saucepan and place his or her palm under it. At first touch the saucepan may be hot. Repeat until the bottom of the saucepan is merely warm to the touch. Stir in the peanut butter. Beat mixture until it is no longer shiny. Pour quickly into the cake pan. Let cool. Ask your adult helper to cut the fudge into squares.